Emma's Cold Day

By Margriet Ruurs
Illustrations by Barbara Spurll

Stoddart
Kids
TORONTO • NEW YORK

To Susan Close, educator extraordinaire.
— M.R.

To the memory of Cheryl May Gee (1947-2001)
— B.S.

Published in Canada in 2001 by
Stoddart Kids,
a division of Stoddart Publishing Co. Limited
895 Don Mills Road, 400-2 Park Centre
Toronto, Ontario M3C 1W3
Tel (416) 445-3333 Fax (416) 445-5967
E-mail cservice@genpub.com

Published in the United States in 2002 by
Stoddart Kids,
a division of Stoddart Publishing Co. Limited
180 Varick Street, 9th Floor
New York, New York 10014
Toll free 1-800-805-1083
E-mail gdsinc@genpub.com

Distributed in Canada by
General Distribution Services
325 Humber College Blvd.,
Toronto, ON M9W 7C3
Tel (416) 213-1919 Fax (416) 213-1917
E-mail cservice@genpub.com

Distributed in the United States by
General Distribution Services
4500 Witmer Industrial Estates, PMB 128
Niagara Falls, New York 14305-1386
Toll free 1-800-805-1083
E-mail gdsinc@genpub.com

National Library of Canada Cataloguing in Publication Data

Ruurs, Margriet, 1952–
Emma's cold day

ISBN 0-7737-3314-0

I. Spurll, Barbara. II. Title.

PS8585.U97E453 2001   jC813'.54   C2001-930584-2
PZ7.T88Ema 2001

*On a frosty winter day, Emma sets out to
solve the problem of a cold chicken coop.*

Special thanks to Erika Bakker's Grade 2 Class at the Vernon Christian School.

THE CANADA COUNCIL | LE CONSEIL DES ARTS
FOR THE ARTS | DU CANADA
SINCE 1957 | DEPUIS 1957

*We acknowledge for their financial support of our
publishing program the Canada Council, the Ontario Arts
Council, and the Government of Canada through the
Book Publishing Industry Development Program (BPIDP).*

Printed and bound in Hong Kong, China
by Book Art Inc., Toronto

Emma sat inside the chicken coop with all the other chickens.
She fitted on her nest like the lid on a cookie jar.

As she began to snooze, Emma heard something strange.
Her beak was chattering all by itself.

Before long, Emma was shivering all over. She got up stiffly
and stretched her skinny legs, trying to get warm. She hopped
up and down, she flapped her wings, but nothing worked.
The hen house was freezing.

All of the other chickens huddled on their nests. Their beaks
were chattering, too.
"Tok!" said Emma. "This isn't good for chickens."
And she set off to find a way to stay warm.

Emma blinked as she stepped outside. The whole world was white. She picked her way across the barnyard. As Emma sank deep into the snow, she noticed the horse on his four long legs. He didn't seem bothered by the cold.

Emma looked down at her own stubby legs. "Tok," she said. "If my legs were longer, maybe I would be warm, too."

Emma fluttered onto the tall fence post, but it was covered with a puff of snow and she slid right off. She took another flying leap. This time she fell beak first into the snow.

The horse watched, looking warm and shaking his head. Emma dusted herself off and plodded away.

Near the barn a flock of sheep stood, bundled in their warm, woolly coats. Emma tried ruffling her feathers and snuggling into her own coat, but her bottom stuck out. She wrapped her wings around herself, but they didn't reach far enough. Emma was still shivering.

"B-a-a-a-a," balked the sheep.

"T-t-t-tok!" chattered Emma, as she strutted off toward the barn.

Inside, huge black and white cows crowded
together, their steamy breath rising in
clouds. "Mmmmmooooohhhh!" the cows
moaned as they munched on their hay.
Maybe this was the way to stay warm.
Emma crowded her way in between the
warm cows.

CRASH! A huge hoof nearly flattened her,
but Emma jumped out of the way.
SWOOSH! A tail almost knocked her into a
cow pie. SLURRRP! The long tongue of
a jigsaw calf gave her a slimy, slobbery lick.

"TOK!" cried Emma. This was worse than
freezing! Carefully, she picked her way out
of the barn and back into the cold.

When Emma came to the pig sty, she peeked in. One huge boar was over by the slop trough. A lo-o-o-ng sow was stretched out in the mud. Ten tiny pink piglets were cuddled against her, grunting and sighing happily. Emma wasn't sure what they were doing, but they looked warm and cozy. Maybe she could be warm and cozy there, too. Emma tiptoed through the muck and wriggled her way in between two piglets.

"Eeeeee!" they squealed, as soon as they felt Emma's feathers against their stubby backs.

"Grumphf!" grunted their mother, as she spotted the intruder.

"Harumpff!" snorted their father, as he charged at Emma.

"*TOK!*" shrieked Emma, and she ran from the pig sty and back into the snow.

Leaving muddy tracks, Emma trotted past the empty turkey pen. She trudged past the pond where the ducks, warm and content, stood sleeping on one leg. "T-t-t-t-t-t-o-k," Emma stuttered. If only this was the way to stay warm. Slowly, she pulled up her right leg and — plopped over into the snow. She scrambled to her feet and tried with her left leg. Plop! She fell over again. The ducks chuckled softly to themselves.

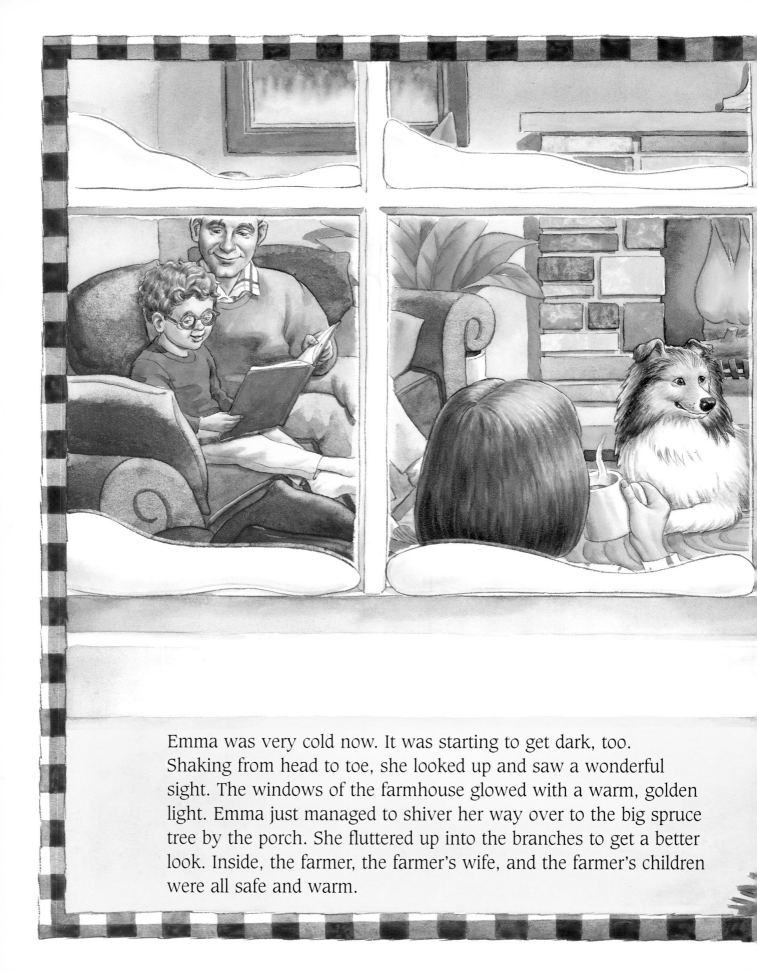

Emma was very cold now. It was starting to get dark, too.
Shaking from head to toe, she looked up and saw a wonderful
sight. The windows of the farmhouse glowed with a warm, golden
light. Emma just managed to shiver her way over to the big spruce
tree by the porch. She fluttered up into the branches to get a better
look. Inside, the farmer, the farmer's wife, and the farmer's children
were all safe and warm.

The green branches of the spruce tree were like a giant nest. Emma was cold. Emma was tired. She snuggled into her feathers and settled down for a little nap. Snowflakes fell softly around her.

Suddenly, Emma was wide awake. A strange green light glowed on the branch beside her. She blinked up at a blue bulb and a radiant red one above her head. There were lights everywhere, and all those lights were melting the snow away. Emma heard children's voices.

"Mom, Dad! There's something in the tree!"

"Is it a partridge in a pear tree?" joked the farmer.

"No!" answered the boy. "It's a chicken in a Christmas tree!"

"It's Emma!" added the girl. "She's sitting underneath the Christmas lights!"

"Poor Emma," cooed the farmer's wife. "She's half frozen. Why ever would she leave her warm chicken coop?"

"Oh, my goodness!" cried the farmer, hurrying away. "I forgot to switch on the heat lamps in the hen house!"

Emma could hear the clacking of cold beaks as she neared the chicken coop. Warmth was just beginning to fill the hen house, when she appeared in the doorway.

"You girls have Emma to thank," said the farmer. "Without her, you would have been pretty chilly chicks by morning!"

"Tok!" said Emma, feeling very proud of herself. The cold day was over. Emma settled down on her nest of straw and dozed happily off to sleep.